AF410504

Prologue

Smoke coming from all sides of a black broken car with a flat tire, as a pair of twins struggled to get out of the car. The fire was getting hotter and ashes were choking them. The burglar who had kidnapped them, had sped away from the road on the cliff where the burning car was, and to the sun that was rising slowly . The little boy in the car ripped off his gag, and started screaming. All of a sudden, he stopped. A tall dead-looking tree that the car had hit, started cracking, and before the twins knew it, had started to pull away from the ground. The boy ducked, but his twin was frozen with fear. She moaned as the tree fell on her, then let out an ear piercing shriek. With a last breath of air, life was sucked out of her as her twin jumped out of the broken

window. Tears streaming out of his emerald green eyes, he laid her against the smoldering car. The boy looked up. A flash of red and blue flashed through the window, and a white police car came to a stop. It had heard the scream. "Don't worry kid," the officer said soothingly, as he jumped off the car. "She can't be dead."
He beckoned the boy over to his side, and helped him climb into the car. Then, he picked up the dead girl, who was as lifeless and pale as marble, and carried her into the back of the car. Her soul was sucked up into the heavens, where our story begins.

Ziggy

The girl was named Ziggy. She had flaming red hair, and green eyes, just like her twin, Zack. Now, she was completely white. Ziggy opened her eyes. She stared around, and blinked. Everything had gone white, even she had gone white. Ziggy had a crazy thought that she was in a parallel universe, where everything was albino. But then the memories came back to her.

She was sleeping. A loud crash woke her up. A terrified Zach looked up at her from the bottom of their bunk bed.

"What's going on?" He cried.

All of a sudden, footsteps reached her ears, and before she knew what was happening, she was getting gagged by a stranger wearing black. They stuffed herself and Zach into bags, and hurried out of the house and into a car. She tried to scream, but choked on the gag. The car started speeding down the road, to a cliff, but hit a tall tree. Fire started springing

Ziggy suddenly knew why she was surrounded by white. She was dead. She stood up and walked around. She touched the ground, and felt that it was just some tufts of cloud. She dug a hole in the ground and looked through it. She saw a building. It was big, black, and slightly creepy. The moment she let go of the soft fluff, it resealed itself. She dug a hole again, and watched a police officer leading a kid with bright red hair through a big open door. Without warning, a staircase appeared beneath her feet, a long spiraling one, leading to a patch of silvery light. Ziggy, still watching through the hole, slipped, and tumbled through the staircase. She closed her eyes, feeling like she would vomit as she rolled down it. When she slid to a stop at the bottom of the staircase, she opened her eyes. The silvery light caught her gaze, and she gently prodded the substance with her fingers. Suddenly, Ziggy felt a whooshing sensation, and she was pulled towards the light. Blinded by the light, she squeezed her eyes shut again, and was transported to a tall black gate, the only thing that was not white. An old man, who was missing a few teeth and albino too, though still dressed very finely - in white of course, appeared out of nowhere, and smiled at her. "Welcome to Heaven," He said kindly, "Come in."

He ushered her through the gate, and her eyes met a beautiful scene - even though it was completely white. There were big, beautiful, iridescent pearls with clear glass windows and doors for houses, and a shining white sun shone in the sky. Under the houses, old and young people were feasting on the finest food, at a long marble table. The food smelled and looked delicious even though it was white. Ziggy's mouth watered.

"You are welcome to eat with us. You've just made it in time for lunch." The old man said.

"There's nowhere for me to sit though..." Muttered Ziggy.

"That is easily fixed!" Said the old man happily, and a table came zooming to meet the bigger one, then, they morphed together.

He grinned at Ziggy, then took his place next to an old woman, no doubt his wife. She waved merrily at Ziggy, then continued to eat. Ziggy sat down and heaped her plate with a bit of everything, and filled her empty cup with a creamy glass of goat's milk. It was delicious, the savory turkey filled her mouth with a taste unrivaled by any other meat. The gravy and cranberries were so mouthwatering, that Ziggy could hardly believe she could have survived without it. The warm milk went down her throat and made her feel calm and satisfied with the world. After lunch, the kind old man and his wife walked Ziggy to the check-in stand. A woman with short hair in her teens looked down a list.

"Ziggy… Ziggy… Yes. Here you are. House 269."

"Thanks!" Ziggy said, as the girl passed her the house keys.

"Come back here if you need a key replacement!" Cried, she cried, waving at Ziggy.

Ziggy looked down at her key and saw a button with the inscription *Press Here.* She pressed the button and was teleported to a house with a sign reading: "269". She turned the knob, and found herself looking at a circular bed, a shower and toilet, bookshelf with a single book on it, a glass table with a white lily on it, a guidebook, a telephone, and a wardrobe. Ziggy put down the key on the table and read the book.

Welcome to Heaven! Here is a map. Press the different buttons to go to different places. On your bookshelf should be a memory book of your life. To borrow books, go to the library.

Mealtimes:

Breakfast: 6:00 - 10:30

Lunch: 11:00 - 1:00

Dinner: 5:00 - 8:00

Ziggy put down the book, and rushed over to the bookshelf. She took the memory book out and saw the status of her family. Mom: Alive, Dad: Alive, Zach: Alive. Ziggy's heart leaped. Zach was still alive. She flipped the page and saw herself and Zach eating popsicles together in the hot summer's sun. The pictures were the only thing colored, in the whole heaven. She smiled sadly.

"I hope you have a wonderful life Zach." She murmured. Ziggy put the book away, and headed towards the wardrobe. Fresh new clothes stood there, waiting for her. She changed into a tee shirt with cotton pants, and then opened the hand book again.

Where should I go today? Ziggy wondered. *I definitely need some books.* So Ziggy pressed the library button, and was immediately transported to the library. Birch bookshelf filled with books lined the library, and Ziggy, delighted, ran over to the fiction side. Picking out no less than ten thick books, she piled them on the librarian's desk.

"Your due date is next year, dear," She said smiling sweetly at Ziggy. "Enjoy!" So later that day, Ziggy lay on her bed, munching on dried fruits, and reading books.
This is paradise, she thought.

Zach

Zack's life however, was far from paradise. In fact, it was near daily torture. Ever since Ziggy had died in the car crash, Zach had been living in a cold, stone orphanage, the one that Ziggy saw. When the lady in the orphanage, who was wearing fine silks, and had a look of eating way to much, had first taken Zach in, she was smiling. But when the police officer left, the woman changed completely.
"To your room!" She thundered, pointing at a door with bars that looked

like a prison cell. Her face, no longer the sweet smiling face, was looking like a saber-toothed tiger. Startled and scared, Zach hurried into the cell with a quick: "Yes ma'am." She locked the door, and as she turned and walked to her fine room that had a blazing fire, Zach distinctively heard her mutter: "Another pampered brat." Zach, cold and tear-stained, sat on a moldy stool, and started to cry.

"Don't cry." A voice said. "We all hate Ms. Nemfis. You know, that fat old woman."

Zach looked around, and saw a boy, about the same age as himself, with short brown hair, and broken, square glasses.

"Who are you?" Zach asked, "I'm Zack."

"I'm James." The boy said grinning.

James lit a match, and a warm fire lit the damp, musty room.

"Hungry?" He asked, pulling out two meat buns for them to share. "Ms. Ada, Ms. Nemfis's sister lives on the other side of the street. She earns a decent amount of money, so she can provide us with food. I dug a hole in the wall so we can sneak up to Ms. Ada's house. She hates Ms. Nemfis too."

"Thanks so much!" Said Zach taking a bite of the delicious meat bun.

They sat in silence, chewing and swallowing the food. After the buns had been demolished, Zach suddenly thought of something.

"How does Ms. Nemfis not notice?" He asked.

"Oh her," James said dismissively, "She doesn't care about us. She just takes children in, and locks us in cells."

"How did you even end up in this place?" Zach asked James.

James sighed. "My dad died when I was 3. My mom couldn't earn enough money, so she brought me to this dump. Then, she died. What about you?"

"I was kidnapped." Zach said, recalling the worst memory of his life. "The burglar drove into a tree, then ran away. My sister got crushed. She didn't duck in time."

Silence fell upon them once more.

"I'm sorry about your sister." James said.

But Zach didn't reply. He was too busy thinking about the kidnapper.

"I think..." he said slowly, "Ms. Nemfis was my kidnapper.

"Well, that would make sense." said James thoughtfully." Ms. Nemfis has done kidnapping before."

Zach gasped. "Who?"

"A pair of twins." James replied. "They were taking a walk outside, when Ms. Nemfis kidnapped them. Very unfortunate. Ms. Nemfis is money hungry, and gets fifty dollars for each kid she takes in. Luckily, Ms. Ada took them in, but that's all the children she could."

"I can't believe she is so evil! Stealing kids for money..." Zach shook his head. He blew out the fire, and they fell asleep under the ragged sheets. Zach dreamed that he and Ziggy were eating popcorn on the doorstep of their cozy house. Their parents were working inside, and a 'click clack' noise came from their house. Zach and Ziggy were trying to toss popcorn into their mouths, when a big, and unpleasant looking woman with curly mousy brown hair, big bulging eyes, and yellow pointed teeth came. She held a knife in one hand, and a black bag in the other. It was Ms. Nemfis. With an evil smile, she threw him in the bag, and drove away. Once she had disposed of him in a cell, she walked away.

"Zach?" Somebody tapped him. "Wake up. Breakfast time."

Zach yawned, and James gave him a pancake. Then, he lit the pile of sticks once more, and they warmed themselves by the fire. It was damp and musty in the cold, and their clothes were ragged and torn, so it felt wonderful to feel warm. After eating, they found some sticks and stones, and played a game of tic-tac-toe. *Maybe, life isn't going to be so bad.* Zach thought.

Ziggy

Ziggy walked down the spiraling staircase of her newly-built treehouse, feeling a bit down. *Heaven is wonderful,* she thought. *Everyone is nice to me, but I need an actual friend. One who will care about me. Just like Zach did.* Ziggy picked up the memory book and flipped through the pages. She strolled down to the check-in station, and asked the nice lady if she could see her brother.

"Of course ," she said. "Lots of people here want to see what's going on with their still-alive family. Just take this card, and go to the gate. Press the name on the card that you want to see, and then you will become a ghost. You will float to whoever you want to see, and press the back button on the card to go back. You can go through walls, and fly."

So Ziggy transformed into a ghost, and was transported to the orphanage.

Zach and Ziggy

Where am I? Ziggy wondered, looking at the big black building that looked familiar. *Most importantly, where is Zach?* She floated through the wall, and gasped. There were hundreds of tiny cells along the long stone wall. Even though she was a ghost, and was comfortably warm, she shivered at the sight of it. What if Zach was in one of them? Ziggy peeked through the bars of the first cell in the line. Two boys were sitting in it, around a small fire. Though Zach's hair was covered in soot, it was still remarkably red. Ziggy felt happy and sad at the sight of Zach. He was alive, but very mistreated.

"Zach?" She whispered.

"Ziggy?" He said, surprised.

The other boy just sat there gaping at her.

"You-you're a ghost! Zach exclaimed.

"Yes," she replied, "I have come to get you and your friend out of here. What is his name again?"

"Yippee! Also, my name is James." Cried James happily. "I better tell Ms. Ada, the nice lady who also happens to be the evil orphanage keeper's sister, when we go and get our food."

Zach felt ecstatic. He was going! He was reunited with Ziggy! Well, sort of. Zach got a napkin Ms. Ada had given him, and wrote down a plan to escape.

"Maybe when we get breakfast tomorrow, Ziggy could lead us to Heaven?" He suggested.

"Possible choice, I can turn solid." Ziggy told him.

"Then it's settled." James said happily, clapping his hands.

Ziggy sighed. "Alive humans can only stay a week at a time in heaven."

"Then we'll visit you a week at a time." James said.
Ziggy grinned. The next day, the boys went over to Ms. Ada's shop, with Ziggy floating behind them. Ms. Ada was delighted that Zach and James could finally escape the orphanage, so much, that she forgot to give them breakfast. As Ziggy pulled them up into the sky, Zach said that Heaven would probably just give them food. What Zach said was proven to be correct, after several minutes, when the two friends went through the advanced technology and did a whole bunch of body scans with it. Then, James spotted the food table, and stuffed his mouth with as many potato chips he could chew. Zach patted James's back as he choked on the seventh chip bag he ate. Both of them were so hungry, they didn't know that everything around them was white, so

Ziggy smirked at them as they stared at the place, their mouths wide open. James gave a loud burp, and a tiny kid sitting on the other side of the table giggled. James wiggled his eyebrows at the kid, who started laughing. Zach started gobbling down piles of mashed potatoes, so fast that the plate had to refill itself. After they ate, James and Zach had eaten so much, they could hardly stand up. Ziggy had to carry them into her room. *Note to self,* she thought, *don't let Zach and James eat too much.* James laid down on the fluffy white bed.

"I haven't slept in a decent bed for years!" he said.

Ziggy was stunned. She could barely say the words: "You haven't slept in a bed for years? Why did the orphanage person do that to you?"

"Mean genes, probably," James said casually, picking up a piece of fruit. "Is this one of those big raisins, or a dried apricot?"

"It's an apricot," Ziggy told him. "Taste it. Anyways, you said the keeper's sister was nice, but you also said that they have evil genes."

"Maybe the mean keeper, Ms. Nemfis, is the first to be evil?" Zach said.

"Possibly…" James muttered, scratching his chin.

Ziggy looked down at the fruit bowl, and saw that half of all the fruit was gone.

"You guys need to establish a better diet." she exclaimed. "Was Ms. Nemfis that bad? Also, I thought Nemfis was a singer."

"Wish she was." Zach mumbled. "Then she'd be nice and wouldn't be our keeper.

They spent the rest of the day at the water park, and James accidentally poked a hole in the sky. Zach had to go to the check in lady and get some glue to repair it, but not before James poked his head through it, and saw Ms. Nemfis. Disgusted at her appearance, and partly because he'd eaten too much, James vomited on her. The rest of the week went smoothly, not counting the several times James got into trouble, one occasion when James accidentally fried a goat by making the sun rays pointing at it, leading to the herd scrambling for good hiding spots, and the receptionist turning back time. *I'll try to make sure James doesn't get into more trouble.* Zack thought. On the last day of their stay, Zach and James waved goodbye at the perfect paradise, and said hello to the the dark, damp orphanage awaiting their arrival.

"I wanna x-ray Ms. Nemfis." Ziggy told them, "Then we'll get rid of her for good." So Ziggy went with them back to the orphanage, carrying a portable high-tech x-ray from the fifth millennium. The receptionist lady had to go into the future, and take it from a store. When they at last got into the orphanage, Ziggy went to invisible ghost mode. She creeped into the warm room, and x-rayed Ms. Nemfis. Memorizing the results, she tiptoed back into the cell.
"Turns out that Ms. Nemfis is half alien, half human. The alien species is some sort of octopus mixed with a cheetah with wings," Ziggy informed them.
"That's how she got into the upstairs room! She flew!" Zach said.
"And that's how she got the Ponaldo twins! She grabbed them from the sea." James added.

"But how can we take her down if she has all sorts of powers?" Ziggy wondered aloud.

"Maybe we'll lure her to tie her tentacles when she's waving them" Zach said.

"Yeah!" James cried. "She'll be tied in her own tentacles!

Ziggy took out a laser gun and fried the cell open. Zach and James ran out, and holding on to Ziggy, flew to Heaven and prepared for a fight. The receptionist gave them some protection, but warned them that Ms. Nemfis may be evil enough to break down Heaven, without the strong protection charms put on it. They took heed of the warning, and raced back to Earth before Ms. Nemfis could kidnap any more kids. First, they sprinted over to Ms. Ada's cafe, and asked her about Ms. Nemfis.

"Ms. Nemfis's mom married a alien man, and they bore a child. But little did

her mom know that he was an alien.
One day, they went broke, and her
husband stole some money. She saw
him in his alien form, and immediately
divorced. Then she married her best
friend, and had me. Ms. Nemfis was
sent to an orphanage, while I was cared
by a family. Years passed, and Ms.
Nemfis grew ruthless, selfish, and
jealous that I had a proper family. So
she started kidnapping children, so
many families would feel the pain she
felt."
"Maybe she isn't all that bad." Ziggy
commented.
"She is, and will never change. If I had
helped her when she was younger, none
of this would have happened." Sighed
Ms. Ada.
The trio ran back to the orphanage,
determined to defeat Ms. Nemfis. Ziggy
pulled out a shrinking bike from her

pocket, and changed to solid form. She pedaled to the police station and informed them about what she was going to do. Sweat trickled down her wet face as she pedaled back as fast as she could, and her face had a look of determination on them. She hopped off the bike, and put it back into her pocket. Then, Ziggy got her laser, and flicked the black switch on. She hurried into the large room where Ms. Nemfis was sitting, her tentacles waving as she tried to move. James and Zach had succeeded in tying her up. Ziggy slashed through her murderers stomach, and Ms. Nemfis crumpled to the ground.

"I c-can't believe it," stammered Ziggy, "I-I killed her."

"No you didn't." An icy voice said. "Don't you remember, cats have nine lives."

James gasped. "Ms. Nemfis is part cheetah which is a type of big cat!"

Ms. Nemfis rose up, her large, leathery wings creating a slight breeze, and her sharp teeth barred.

"I won't kill anyone." She said, her menacing voice making a chill creep up Ziggy's spine. "I need the money from the police. I need you all to learn how to suffer. And I will get my revenge."

She curled a tentacle around Ziggy's waist.

"You. You cannot die anymore. You have access to Heaven. Come join me. Do not resist the powerful force of the darkside, or you will suffer. Come to me."

Ziggy closed her eyes shut. Pain Ziggy had never felt was stabbing at her like daggers slashing her whole body. She couldn't die, but she could suffer. She couldn't join Ms. Nemfis. Even if she suffered for all eternity, no matter how much she wanted, she couldn't. But a voice spoke in the back of her head. *Join her. The pain will cease immediately. Join the darkside.*

"Never!" Ziggy cried, breaking free of Ms. Nemfis's grasp, and falling to the floor.

"Ziggy!" Zach gasped.

"Zach..." She moaned.

Zach's hatred towards Ms. Nemfis strengthened. He wasn't going to let her sister suffer because of that evil lady. James picked up a dagger from the floor and looked at the dark red blood. The blood of innocent parents Ms. Nemfis had killed. James patted Zach on the shoulder, with a sad smile. James's qwips were gone. His smiles, his burps, all gone. James slashed at all the cell bars, freeing all the children trapped in there. The children ran towards Ms.

Nemfis. Hatred burned in all of their eyes. They set her on fire, punched her with their puny fists, and tied her to a burning pole. Ziggy suddenly awoke, and slashed Ms. Nemfis once again. She crumpled to the ground, truly dead. The police tossed her into a capsule making sure she wouldn't awake again.

But her soul went out of the capsule. It squeezed Ziggy. Ziggy again felt the pain. Oh! She couldn't resist it. She squirmed, but would not give in. Never. The dark demon pulled her to Hell, where Ms. Nemfis would suffer eternally.

Now, Ziggy lives in Heaven, where she visits her brother and his friend James everyday. No story can end unhappily, right? Zach and James lived at Zach's home, where James was cared for, by his new parents.

Now

The sun was warming the steps of the steps of a butter colored house, where two kids and a ghost were playing with a puppy. The girl was Ziggy, who was the ghost. The first boy was James, and the second was Zach. Ziggy had gotten her dream. Now she had a friend, who cared for her just like Zach did. James was his name, and he was also Ziggy's brother. He was adopted by Zach and Ziggy's Mum and Dad. The children in the orphanage were cared for in proper homes, and went to actual schools. The burnt ruins of the old orphanage was made into a big school, with a fancy library, and of course, the laser Ziggy had use to end Ms. Nemfis.
They flew to Heaven for their annual 'No more Evil Alien Nemfis' party. Once they got there, James tore off the wax wings he used to fly. He poked a big hole in the wall of Heaven protection.

He looked inside, and saw Ms. Nemfis screaming.

"Jeepers!" He cried, "She sure is loud!" James stuck his head inside, and accidentally slipped inside. Zach and Ziggy who were still holding on to him, slid down too.

"Darn it!" Zach told him. "We are stuck!"